STAR-CROSSED

STAR-CROSSED

LOREN BAILEY

DARBY CREEK

MINNEAPOLIS

Darby Creek
A division of Lerner Publishing Group, Inc.
241 First Avenue North
Minneapolis, MN 55401 USA

For reading levels and more information, look up this title at www.lernerbooks.com.

Image credits: kutaytanir/Getty Images; lazy clouds/Shutterstock.com; art of line/Shutterstock.com; Alexander Lysenko/Shutterstock.com; andvasiliev/Shutterstock.com; Siarhei Tolak/Shutterstock.com; STILLFX/Shutterstock.com; MarijaPiliponyte/Shutterstock.com; Rebellion Works/Shutterstock.com.

Main body text set in Janson Lt Std 12/17.5.
Typeface provided by Adobe Systems.

Library of Congress Cataloging-in-Publication Data

Names: Bailey, Loren, author.
Title: Star-crossed / Loren Bailey.
Description: Minneapolis : Darby Creek, [2019] | Series: AI High | Summary: Partnered for a school project intended to improve android/human relations, a human girl and an android boy develop feelings for each other even though their families object.
Identifiers: LCCN 2018040449 (print) | LCCN 2018047147 (ebook) | ISBN 9781541556942 (eb pdf) | ISBN 9781541556904 (lb : alk. paper)
Subjects: | CYAC: Robots—Fiction. | Dating (Social customs)—Fiction. | Prejudices—Fiction. | High schools—Fiction. | Schools—Fiction.
Classification: LCC PZ7.1.B326 (ebook) | LCC PZ7.1.B326 St 2019 (print) | DDC [Fic]—dc23

LC record available at https://lccn.loc.gov/2018040449

Manufactured in the United States of America
1-46124-43499-1/22/2019

TO MY FAMILY—FOR ENCOURAGING ME,
FOR LOVING ME, FOR NOT QUESTIONING
MY SANITY WHEN I CHANGED MY MAJOR
TO ENGLISH LITERATURE

SIX MONTHS AGO, THE US GOVERNMENT OFFICIALLY RECOGNIZED A GROUP OF ANDROIDS WITH ARTIFICIAL INTELLIGENCE AS A RACE OF LIVING BEINGS. These androids look exactly like humans—except for their glowing purple eyes. They have even been built to age like real humans. The first generation of adult androids have combined their programming to produce a second generation of androids: teenagers, kids, and even babies. They aren't entirely machine or entirely human but somewhere in between.

Originally, androids lived in shacks on the outskirts of towns. Recently, the government offered them housing in sectioned-off neighborhoods. Humans are upset about being displaced from their homes, and androids are frustrated that human police officers are patrolling their new neighborhoods. Protests have turned violent. Riots have broken out in the streets.

In an effort to help androids and humans coexist, the government has launched a pilot program for android students in several high schools across the country. One of those high schools is Fitzgerald High School, nicknamed AI High.

Now, about eight hundred teen androids—almost one-fifth of the school population—attend Fitzgerald High. Android students take classes to learn about living in human society. Humans and androids also take classes together in hopes of building understanding and harmony. But many from both sides are reluctant about this new program.

With the teenage androids participating in a school system for the first time in their lives and the tension between the groups simmering, every day brings uncertainty.

1

ALYSSA

Alyssa Collins strummed her fingers nervously against her desk, waiting for her name to be called. It was the first day of school—the first day of this new program.

As the teachers standing in front of the classroom rattled off name after name, Alyssa looked around her. Half the students sitting among her were familiar faces. Everyone in this class was a junior at Fitzgerald High—or AI High, which is what everyone called it now—and Alyssa had known most of them since kindergarten. Many of them stared blankly ahead, as if this were a first day like

3

any other. Some shifted anxiously in their seats like she did. And some didn't even try to hide their glares at the remaining half of the class.

Androids. Transferred in to whatever grade lined up with their age, even though android kids hadn't attended any school up until now. Everyone had to take this Android/Human Relations class. At least the class was separated by grade. Taking a class with a new group of living beings was one thing, but having to do it with a bunch of annoying freshmen and sophomores seemed like torture.

"Carla Diaz," Mrs. Murphy, the human teacher of the class, read from the tablet in her hand. Carla slowly raised her hand.

"And Simone Green," finished Ms. Scarlet, the class's android teacher. The two teachers stood at the front of the room together, sharing the authority of the class. They seemed to be the only ones in the room comfortable with the idea of this program.

An android sitting in the front row raised her hand. She looked over her shoulder to where Carla still had hers in the air. Their eyes met and they sized each other up silently. When neither said anything, the teachers continued through their list.

Alyssa rocked in her seat, wishing her name would get called already.

She huffed out a breath when yet another human name was called that wasn't hers. They'd gone through nearly the entire class by now, so she had to be up soon. It wasn't that she had a problem with the androids joining their school, nor did she mind that she would be partnered with an android student in this class for the entire semester.

What bothered Alyssa was the fact that none of the android names that had been called so far were Reid Black.

At the thought of him, Alyssa found herself peeking over her shoulder at an android boy sitting in the back of the classroom. He seemed harmless enough, staring down at something on his desk as if he weren't even listening to the names being called out. If she hadn't known better, she would have thought he was human. His dark, curly hair was slightly messy like many other boys' in her school. He wore black jeans and a plaid shirt like other boys wore. He was so tall that his legs stuck out awkwardly from beneath his desk, but other boys were tall too. But then his gaze flicked up, as if he'd felt her stare, and she found a pair of glowing *purple* eyes looking back at her.

Alyssa jumped and quickly faced forward again. Her heart pounded in her chest, but she reminded herself that he probably had no idea who she was. She knew who he was, though. Her stepdad, John, was a police officer. When the androids were first declared a living race six months ago, John had helped with the relocation process that moved all the androids into neighborhoods set aside specifically for them. It hadn't been an easy process. Alyssa had heard story after story from John about androids that put up a fight about the relocation.

The worst stories, though, were about Derek Black. She'd never actually met him, but she'd seen him on the news. He was about ten years older than her, so he was in between the first generation of androids and this younger generation that was part of the new school program. And he did *not* like humans. Countless times these past six months, John had come home complaining about how he or another officer had broken up yet another fight between androids and humans that had been started by Derek Black.

John had never mentioned Derek's younger brother being there, but she figured Reid was equally bad news. Her last name was different than John's, so even if the Black brothers knew who her stepdad was, they wouldn't think to connect him to her. Still, Alyssa figured she would rather be partnered with any android in this class besides Reid.

There were only a handful of students left to be partnered up by now. She looked up at the clock. How had class only started fifteen minutes ago? This was going to be the longest day of the year.

Alyssa fought the urge to glance around the classroom again, wondering how many androids were left that hadn't been paired up.

There were about thirty students in the room—surely most of them had already been called. Meaning . . .

"Alyssa Collins," Mrs. Murphy said, jolting Alyssa out of her thoughts.

Oh no, she thought.

"And," Ms. Scarlet continued, "Reid Black."

2
REID

After everyone had been partnered up, the teachers told the students to find their partners and push their desks together so the class would be seated in pairs.

Most of the students simply sat there at first. It wasn't until Mrs. Murphy smacked a hand on the desk of a human boy sitting in the front row and yelled, "Chop chop!" (*one of the humans' many odd phrases*, Reid thought to himself) that some of the students hesitantly approached their partners.

Reid didn't know any of the human students, but he'd managed to figure out who his partner would be before her name had even been called. It was a simple calculation of probability that hadn't even really required the advanced programming of his mind. He'd watched as she'd stiffened at the sound of his name, keeping her hand raised as if it were painful to do so. He'd seen her staring at him earlier. He may not have had much experience with humans, but it was easy to figure out that she was nervous. Maybe even afraid of androids.

So he decided to sit at his desk and do nothing. Let her come to him. He wanted to see what she would do.

She stubbornly stayed put at first, although about half the class had done the same. He found himself wondering what she was waiting for. He couldn't stop watching her. She had long, dark hair and dark eyes, and, from what he knew of humans, the sprinkle of freckles across her face was fairly uncommon. Still, there was something besides her distinctive features that made him unable to look away from her.

Finally the human girl rose from her seat. She squared her shoulders and walked over to him.

Her eyes had barely passed over him before she looked down at Patrick, the android sitting next to him. The majority of androids were, at best, hesitant about this new socialization program, but Patrick and his family were some of the few who were completely against humans and androids joining together. He sat in his desk and glared at any human who'd looked his way. When the human girl—*Alyssa*, Reid reminded himself—came their way, Patrick's glare only intensified.

Alyssa glared right back at him, and Reid was surprised to find himself holding in a laugh. "Well?" she snapped. "I'm not dragging my desk all the way over here."

Patrick snorted, but he glanced over at Reid. Patrick's older brother was in Derek's group, and apparently Patrick had decided the two of them would stick together as well. Reid jerked his head, signaling for Patrick to get up. He wasn't going to cause problems on the very first day, and he didn't want Patrick to either.

Patrick scowled as he stood, but he did eventually walk over to his human partner, practically dragging his feet as he did. Alyssa stared at the empty desk, and Reid figured he owed her since she *had* made the first move. He yanked the desk closer to him so they were sitting in a pair like the other students were. She lowered herself to the seat, staring ahead silently.

"All right, everyone," Ms. Scarlet said after everyone had finally gotten settled. "Get comfortable, because these are your seats for the rest of the semester."

Some students groaned. Others shifted in obvious *dis*comfort.

"We don't want to hear it," Mrs. Murphy raised her voice. Everyone quieted, and she gave a calm smile. "Now, your ongoing assignment for the semester is to get to know your partner."

"Find out how you're alike and how you're different," Ms. Scarlet continued. "At the end of the semester, you'll each give a presentation about your partners and what you've learned about the other's culture. Spend these next few months learning about each other—your hobbies, your interests, your families."

Out of the corner of his eye, he saw Alyssa stiffen. She swallowed so heavily he could hear it. Maybe he didn't need this class—the various physical reactions she'd given since they'd been paired told him plenty. Did she really have this much of a problem with androids?

Mrs. Murphy glanced at the clock. "We'd like you to use the rest of class to introduce yourselves. Start thinking about how you'd like to present your projects. It can be an essay, a video, a rap—whatever you want."

With that, she and Ms. Scarlet let the class be. A couple pairings seemed more comfortable with each other and began talking right away.

At first, Reid was perfectly content to sit back and say nothing. He observed the other students in the class, curious about how this program would work out overall. But after a few minutes of silence from his partner,

13

he finally turned to her. He noticed she was sitting as far on the other side of her seat as she could be. "You don't have to sit like that," he said. "I don't bite."

Alyssa let out a huff as she adjusted her position so she was more centered in her seat. "I'm not—it's not . . . *that*," she hissed. "I just didn't know if I would get, like, shocked or something if I got too close."

Reid couldn't help but bark out a laugh. "What, you think we're constantly buzzing with electricity?"

She shrugged, her cheeks turning red as she kept her gaze on her desk.

"You haven't interacted with androids before this, have you?"

She didn't say anything.

"Am I the first android you've ever spoken to?"

"No," she said, looking up at him. "But I haven't really known any personally."

He watched her. He didn't know what else to say, and she seemed perfectly fine with riding out the rest of the class period in silence.

The bell rang, and most of the students practically leapt out of their seats at the sound. The two teachers called goodbye to everyone over the chatter as the others filed out of the room.

Alyssa hurried away without another word to him. As Reid stood, he saw both teachers were watching. He could have sworn they were trying to hold back smiles.

3
REID

The next morning's class period was pretty much the same as the first one. Alyssa sat next to him in near complete silence, barely even looking over at him. The teachers had greeted everyone when the first bell rang, but then like yesterday they stayed quiet at the front of the room and let the student pairs interact with each other. Reid wondered how long they were going to keep that up. Most of the students were more talkative today than they had been yesterday, but his own partner was still noticeably quiet. Halfway through the period, she'd actually taken out a notebook and started working on some algebra problems.

With only a couple minutes left in the class period, Reid finally asked, "So are we going to ignore each other for the entire semester?"

From the way Alyssa was staring down at her notebook, Reid figured she hadn't heard him. He was about to lean in closer and repeat himself when she mumbled, "I'll probably just write a paper or something."

He turned to her. "You're going to write a paper about me without actually speaking to me? Some partnership."

She glared up at him. "Oh, like you really care—"

"Reid, Alyssa," Ms. Scarlet interrupted as she and Mrs. Murphy approached their desks. "Have you two decided on what you'll be doing for your assignment?"

Alyssa actually looked guilty at the question.

"You know, Alyssa, Reid is an incredibly talented photographer," Ms. Scarlet said. "Maybe the two of you could do something with photography." He narrowed his eyes and shook his head at her. Sure he liked photography, but it wasn't necessarily something he wanted to share with a complete stranger—a human one at that—just for a school assignment.

Before he could say anything, Mrs. Murphy jumped in. "That's a wonderful idea. We don't have any photography projects yet." She smiled at them. "Why don't you both take, say, five photos of the other? Try to capture key aspects of each other's lives—what makes both of you who you are."

"I love it," Ms. Scarlet said, typing it into her tablet.

This can't be happening, Reid thought.

"We can take them all here at school, right?" Alyssa asked.

Mrs. Murphy frowned. "I suppose you could, but that doesn't really get into everything about you, does it?"

"Whatever," Alyssa said. "I'll make it work."

"I know you like to write, Alyssa," Mrs. Murphy continued. "Why don't you write titles and captions for each photo? That way you both bring a hobby into the project."

Reid hoped Alyssa would say something to change this plan. Even ignoring each other for the rest of the semester was better than this. "Fine," was all she said.

He scowled.

"Then it's settled," Ms. Scarlet said. "I can't wait to see how it turns out." Mrs. Murphy nodded in agreement.

The teachers moved on to the next partnership, leaving Reid and Alyssa to sit in silence yet again. Reid went over the conversation that had just happened in his mind. He really didn't want to do photography for this project.

He thought about trying to get Alyssa to agree to change their project, but before he could, the bell rang. Alyssa loaded her notebook into her backpack and jumped out of her seat. For a moment he almost wondered if humans had super speed, because even though their desks were in the back of the room she was practically the first person out the door.

* * *

By the end of the day, Reid was more than ready to get out of school. The rigid structure of an eight-hour day took getting used to.

After loading up his backpack, he met up with Patrick and a couple other androids as they were walking out.

The halls were bustling with students, and it almost seemed like a normal high school. But Reid didn't need advanced eyesight to notice the way the human students in the hallway moved away from their group as he and his friends walked past. It was only day two, so most of the students were still staying close to their own kind.

They rounded a corner, and one of his friends crashed into someone. First Reid saw the backpack slide in front of them. He heard the unmistakable slap of human hands smacking onto the tile floor. And then he noticed that the person who'd tumbled backward from the collision was Alyssa.

Her eyes widened when they landed on him.

Patrick let out a cruel laugh. "Can't you watch where you're going, meat bag?

Or do those human eyes of yours not work so well?"

Alyssa ignored him and the others as they laughed. She got to her knees and tried to pick up her backpack, when one of the other androids stepped on the strap that was near his foot. She jerked the bag up before she realized it, and as the strap caught, the backpack yanked open, sending all her books and things pouring onto the floor.

The others cracked up again. "Wow, Reid, they gave you a real winner for that class project," Patrick sneered, elbowing him. Reid hadn't been sure at first, but now he knew that Patrick was doing this because she'd snapped at him yesterday in class.

Alyssa looked up at Reid, as if she too wanted to see what he would do about this. Reid noticed some of the humans who were still lingering in the hall were watching them, uncertain of what to do. He didn't know what to do himself, so he stood there, hands in his pockets. Alyssa glared at him, then ducked to collect her things from the floor.

"Come on," Reid said. "Let's get to the bus. I don't want to have to walk home." It was all he could think to do to get them to leave her alone. He didn't know how Patrick or the others would react if he actually stood up for her. This was the best he could do—or at least that's what he told himself.

But as they passed Alyssa and continued down the hall, he couldn't stop himself from peering back at her. She paused in loading her bag, and the look she gave him lingered in his mind for the rest of the day.

4
ALYSSA

By the time their Android/Human Relations class began the next morning, Alyssa was fully prepared to ignore Reid for the rest of the semester—the rest of the year even. All of high school, for all she cared. She would write a paper as she'd first said, and that would be that. After this class, she would do everything she could to avoid him.

It *did* give her some kind of satisfaction to see him looking so guilty when they both sat down. She pretended she didn't even notice him, but she could see from the corner of her eye that he was watching her, waiting for her to say something to him about what had happened yesterday afternoon.

Alyssa was planning to treat this class as a study hall to finish some of her homework for other classes, but to her surprise the teachers had an actual research assignment for the class today besides just talking to each other.

The students got up to grab tablets to do their research. Alyssa pointedly retrieved only one for herself, and she smirked when Reid quietly huffed to himself as he got up to grab his own.

When Reid sat back down, he continued watching her as she scrolled through one of the news sites listed on the board at the front of the room. He sighed. "Come on," he said finally. "Are you really going to—"

"I've changed my mind about our project," Alyssa interrupted, keeping her eyes on her tablet. She kept her voice light and casual and hoped it grated his nerves. "I'm going back to writing a paper."

"This again?" Reid said. "How are you going to write a whole paper on me? You don't know anything about me."

She whipped her head up to look at him as she said, "I know you made me come to you when we were first partnered up, even though there was an empty seat next to me, which tells me you're arrogant. You chose to sit in the back row, which tells me you don't care about being here. You did nothing to help me yesterday, which tells me you're a jerk."

"Look, I'm—"

"And," she continued, "I know who your brother is, so I know *exactly* what kind of person you are."

He looked as if he hadn't been expecting that. "You may know who my brother is," he hissed, "but that doesn't mean you know anything about *me*."

"What's going on, you two?" Ms. Scarlet asked, coming over to them. It wasn't until Alyssa saw the look on her face that she realized everyone in the class was staring at them.

"Everyone back to work!" Mrs. Murphy said from the front of the room.

"Sorry, Ms. Scarlet," Alyssa said quietly. She could feel her face heating up. "I didn't realize . . ."

"Everything all right?" Ms. Scarlet asked.

Alyssa was tempted to ask for a new partner, but Reid's words rang through her head. *That doesn't mean you know anything about me.*

Reid looked over at Alyssa, as if he was waiting for her to tell Ms. Scarlet what had happened yesterday. Alyssa's mouth went dry, and she found herself unable to say anything.

"It's my fault," he said then, keeping his eyes on Alyssa. "I *was* a jerk. I should have done something yesterday, and I'm sorry."

This time he did look up at their teacher as he repeated Alyssa's words, "Sorry, Ms. Scarlet. We'll keep it down."

Maybe Reid wasn't involved in all the trouble his brother was, like she'd assumed.

"Yeah, we'll keep it down," was all she said.

Ms. Scarlet watched her for another moment before giving them a small smile and returning to the front of the classroom.

Alyssa and Reid got through their assignment for the day easily enough. Though they still didn't speak much, the silence between them was more comfortable. They showed each other different articles and occasionally commented on what they found as they jotted down notes.

They finished with time to spare, and then the tense awkwardness flooded between them again. Alyssa chewed on the side of her lip, watching the clock. Just because they'd gotten through one assignment together didn't mean she wasn't desperate for the class to be over already. She was still annoyed with him.

"Look, I really am sorry about yesterday," he said.

"Mhmm," she said quietly.

"I didn't know they were going to do that— not that it's any excuse—but then I didn't know what to do. And that's not really an excuse either. I just . . ."

Alyssa glanced up at him. "You didn't want to embarrass yourself in front of your friends," she said. "I get it."

"No, that's not it," Reid insisted. "But I know I screwed up. Look, what if I make it up to you?"

She arched an eyebrow at him.

"What if we shoot my photo first? I'll take you somewhere that . . . means something to me."

Alyssa couldn't help herself. "Where is it?"

He grinned mischievously at her. "You'll have to come with me to find out."

5
ALYSSA

Reid refused to tell Alyssa where they were going ahead of time, so she had to drive while he gave her directions. Within minutes, they'd driven to the edge of the human side of town. He instructed her to park on the street, then he climbed out of the car, taking his camera case with him.

Alyssa's stomach clenched when she realized he was leading her to a location on foot. She glanced around. No one else was in the area—no one would see them walking. It wasn't like this was a bad part of town, but it wasn't an area she was familiar with.

Still, as Reid turned back to her and looped his camera strap around his neck, Alyssa found that she wasn't so scared after all. She jogged to catch up with him. "You're not planning to murder me, are you?"

Reid laughed. "Of course not. This spot is way too out in the open," he joked. He gestured toward what she realized used to be an entry gate. Walls of cinderblocks encased the rusted chain-link gate. "Almost there."

The gate wasn't even locked. Reid pushed it open easily, waving Alyssa through.

"We're not, like, trespassing, are we?" she asked. "I don't know if that's going to fly, even for a school project."

He laughed again, shaking his head. "Relax. This place is abandoned." He led her past what looked like had once been a concession stand. When they rounded it, Alyssa spotted rows of parking spots with small speakers next to them. Toward the front of the parking spots were two tall, metal towers, and Alyssa could picture the screen that had once hung between them. She knew where they were.

"A drive-in movie theater?"

Reid nodded. "I used to come here all the time as a kid. It closed down ten years ago."

"I never even knew this was here."

He led her to a picnic table, and they both sat on the table with their feet on the bench. Reid leaned forward to rest his forearms on his knees, letting her take in the space around them. The quiet made Alyssa feel awkward again, so she teased, "So, what, did you have your first date here or something?"

Reid didn't bother answering that. "This is one of the first memories I have of seeing humans," he said quietly. Alyssa felt things shift into seriousness. He stared straight ahead as he continued. "We didn't see many movies when we were little. But I remember coming here with my family for the first time when I was a kid. Some old black and white movie was on the screen. I saw humans on the screen, and then I noticed all the human families in the cars around us. And they were just like us. Watching the movie, laughing, spending time together as a family.

"It was one of the first times I thought that maybe we weren't so different after all. And then, one of the kids in the car next to us looked over, and they all saw my eyes. The parents freaked out. I think they even tried to get us kicked out." He shook his head. "I don't really remember, but I do remember the night was ruined for me either way. It was also the first time I'd seen someone react to me like that."

"I'm sorry," Alyssa said quietly.

"My parents wouldn't come back here," he continued. "That one time was enough for them. But I kept wanting to go back, so my brother would bring me here."

The words Alyssa had said about his brother flashed through her mind. "That was nice of him."

"We would wear sunglasses coming in so the humans wouldn't notice us. And from then on we always parked in the back row," Reid said. "Couldn't see very well, but my brother knew it meant a lot to me to come here."

Alyssa swallowed. "I'm sorry about what I said about him. I shouldn't have—"

"It's fine," he said. "I'm used to it. And just because he was nice to me growing up doesn't really change what kind of person he is now." He glanced over at her. "You know at least something about what he does with his friends. I want you to know that I'm not—I don't do any of that with them."

She didn't know why, but she believed him. "Thank you," she said, "for sharing this with me."

He shrugged.

She smiled shakily at him. "Well, let's take this photo already."

He set up the camera on a tripod and showed her how to use it. Alyssa told him to sit on the picnic table again, and she stood on the other side so she could get the photo over his shoulder with the abandoned drive-in behind him. "Think about that first night again," she told him.

The look on his face wasn't quite as genuine this time, as if he didn't want to show all that emotion again, but Reid stared out ahead of him again and Alyssa snapped the photo. She stared at it in the viewing screen of the camera.

"How is it?" Reid asked.

His profile was striking, she decided as she looked at the image. Not that she was going to tell him that. "It's, uh, it's good," she said quietly. She would call the photo *Drive-In Memories.*

Reid didn't say much as they packed up and walked out of the drive-in. Alyssa wrung her fingers, glancing over at him. "So, you're into photography, huh?" she tried, hoping to pull him out of the dark mood that had taken over him.

"Yeah. I took a lot of photos where we used to live."

They passed through the front gate, and Alyssa still didn't know how to lighten the mood. She looked over at him once again, this time noticing the way his purple eyes had a slight glow to them. "You know, for some reason I'd first thought you would take photos with your . . ."

He looked at her curiously, and she felt her cheeks heat up. "Never mind," she said.

"It's stupid."

Reid smiled crookedly. "Tell me."

"I don't know why, but I guess I figured you, like, took photos with your . . ."

"My . . . ?" he pressed.

"Eyes?" She waved a hand toward his face. "Cause of the, I don't know, computers and stuff?"

Reid burst out laughing. "No," he said. "We're androids, not walking digital media centers. I don't have a 3D printer in my arm." He rolled up his sleeve to reveal a very normal-looking forearm.

If it were possible, Alyssa's face heated even more. "Well, I figured *that*," she insisted. "I just didn't know if—oh, never mind!" She turned away from him and he chuckled, but less than a minute later she found herself peeking down to look at his arm again.

He seemed to notice her staring at him and arched an eyebrow. Alyssa huffed and crossed her arms, but she couldn't even pretend to be annoyed. Not when she'd managed to bring back that playful grin of his.

6
REID

For her first photo, Alyssa had decided she
wanted them to go to her house. Reid was a bit
surprised, since she'd said she would only do
the photos at the school, but he figured after
his photo that maybe she'd decided it was all
right for them to get a little more personal. In
the past week since the drive-in, things had
been . . . different between them. Friendly,
even. He found himself looking forward to
seeing her in class every day.

They picked a day for Reid to ride home
with Alyssa after school. They spoke easily in
the car together. Reid had never been to this

part of town before. It was different from his own neighborhood. The streets were quiet, the houses taken care of. He felt a weird pang and realized it was jealousy—jealousy at what she'd had for a childhood.

"This is it," Alyssa said quietly and stopped her car in front of a house. The house was small, but it looked comfortable. Reid already knew it was just Alyssa, her mom, and her stepdad.

Alyssa cleared her throat, and Reid wondered if she was nervous. "My mom is home, but my stepdad is still at work. He should be in later though." He didn't know why but it seemed like she was telling him this for some specific reason, so he nodded.

As they climbed out, a car sped down the street behind them and turned into the driveway of the house next door. "Come on," Alyssa said, leading him up her own driveway, "we can set our stuff down inside."

A teenage boy got out of the car and slammed the door shut. Reid didn't know him, but he wore what Reid recognized as their school's letterman jacket for football.

"Hey, Alyssa," the guy called to her with a smirk.

Alyssa didn't even turn to him as she waved a hand and said back, "Austin."

They kept walking toward her house, but Reid could tell when Austin noticed his eyes by the way he froze where he stood.

"Is that a *droid*?" he shouted. "What the—"

"Keep your voice down!" Alyssa snapped. Reid noticed her glancing around, as if she was worried about neighbors hearing there was an android with her. She hadn't seemed concerned about that before, but now he wondered if she was.

Austin stalked across the grass of their two yards. He didn't even acknowledge Reid as he glared at Alyssa. "You're bringing one of them to your house? So, what, you're into droids now?"

Reid tensed as Austin said the offensive name for androids—for the second time now—but Alyssa stepped in before he could say anything. "Oh, shut up," she said. "We're working on a class project together."

Austin apparently didn't have anything to

say to that, so he turned his attention back to Reid, sizing him up. Reid returned the glare.

Austin crossed his arms then. "Your stepdad is gonna *love* this," he said. He looked at Alyssa again, his eyes darting up and down. "I'll be out in the back if you need anything."

She snorted. "I think we'll be fine. Let's go, Reid." Then she grabbed his wrist and tugged him to follow her inside.

As they passed through the front door, Reid glanced behind him to see Austin stomping off. "Nice neighbor," he said.

Alyssa rolled her eyes at him. "We grew up together," she said. "He's just . . . protective of me."

"He likes you."

"Yeah, well, he's an idiot." They stopped in the front hall, and Alyssa looked up at him. "I'm sorry he called you that."

Reid shrugged. "It's not the first time I've heard it. Won't be the last, either."

"That doesn't mean it's okay."

Alyssa brought him deeper into her house, where they found her mother in the kitchen.

She was furiously typing away on a laptop at the table, and at first she didn't even look up at them. "Hey, honey, I'm just finishing this report."

"Um, Mom, you remember that I'm working on that class project today, right?" Alyssa interrupted. "This is Reid."

Her mom's fingers paused on the keyboard for a moment before she looked over at them. Her eyes fixated on Reid's. "That's right," she said finally, giving an overly wide smile.

Reid had wondered if Alyssa had given her parents a heads up that she was bringing an android home, and it seemed that there had definitely been some kind of conversation about him.

"Hello! It is so nice to meet you," Alyssa's mom said loudly and slowly, as if he wouldn't be able to understand her. "Welcome to our home—"

"Oh my god, Mom," Alyssa hissed, racing across the kitchen to grab her mom by the arm. She stood with her back to Reid as she whispered, "What are you doing? He speaks

English, and his hearing is perfectly fine. Probably better than either of ours."

"Well, I'm sorry!" her mom whispered back. "How was I supposed to know?" They stared at each other in some kind of silent battle of wills before Alyssa turned around and smiled at him expectantly.

He got the hint. "It's nice to meet you, Mrs. Collins," he said. He was proud of himself for showing human manners, hoping that would work in his favor.

Judging by the looks on their faces, it didn't.

Alyssa coughed. "It's actually Radley," she explained. "Since my mom remarried."

Oh, right, he thought. She'd mentioned she had a stepdad. Androids hadn't really been around long enough for divorce and remarriage, so he wasn't as familiar with this human custom.

"Anyway," Alyssa said brightly, saving him, "we should get to work on our project. We'll just be in my room . . ."

She shoved him toward a closed door down the hall from the kitchen. As Reid opened the door, Alyssa's mother called after her. He paused at the doorway when he was out of sight, curious.

"What is it?" Alyssa asked.

"Keep your door open," her mom said quietly.

"*Mom!*" Alyssa whisper-shouted. "I told you, it's for a project. For school!"

"I know that," her mom said. "But, android or not, he's still a boy."

Whatever Alyssa said in response, he couldn't quite make it out, as she'd hissed it so quietly and so quickly. Reid could just see the shade of red her face must have turned. He laughed—it was actually pretty cute when she got all flustered like that.

* * *

After chatting in her room for a while, they took Alyssa's photo on the swing set in her backyard. Reid had wanted to come up with the title this time, but all he could think of was *Girl on Swings Stares at Nothing*. Alyssa told him he was officially banned from titling privileges.

They were still laughing about it when they came inside through the back door. Reid followed Alyssa into the kitchen, but then she suddenly froze and he bumped into her.

"Hey, human, watch the camera," he teased as he lifted it from where it hung at his chest. He was glad the strap was around his neck, because when he looked up he nearly dropped the camera.

Reid's jaw dropped at the sight of the man wearing a dark uniform standing across from them. *Her stepdad is a . . . cop?* he thought. He immediately tensed up, unable to help the instant reaction to seeing a human police officer. Where he came from, the sight of one only meant trouble. He tried to remind himself that this was his friend's home.

"John," Alyssa said, "this is Reid Black." John's eyebrows shot up at that, and Reid wondered if the man knew of his family. Alyssa didn't seem to notice as she continued. "He's a boy from my school."

John didn't even look at Alyssa. He just continued staring at Reid. "A *boy?*" he questioned. Reid was sure John was assessing his android eyes.

"You know what I mean," Alyssa said. "We're working on a class project together."

Reid noticed her mom standing off to the side, her hands gripping the counter as if she was waiting for something drastic to happen. Alyssa looked back at him, and he cleared his throat. "Nice to meet you, Officer Radley."

He held his hand out for John to shake, but the man only grunted at him. "What's that brother of yours up to tonight?"

Well that answers my question, Reid thought. He pulled his hand back to himself. "I don't know, sir. We came straight here after school."

John's eyes narrowed at him, then flicked over to Alyssa. "It's almost dinnertime. You should wrap up for tonight."

"We took my car here," she said, stepping toward Reid. "I'll just drive him home and—"

"You are *not* going into one of those neighborhoods," John said in a low voice.

"He can't just walk from here," Alyssa insisted.

Her mom stepped forward. "John," she said quietly, "it's just a ride home."

John stared at Reid again, and he felt himself being sized up all over again. His hands were shaking, but he forced himself to hold his chin high and keep eye contact.

"Fine," John said eventually. "But just to the edge of the neighborhood." His eyes shot over to Reid again. "If she's not home within twenty minutes—"

"I will be, I promise," Alyssa insisted. "I'll be fine." She grabbed her bag and keys and tugged Reid behind her. They didn't say a word to each other as she dragged him to her car. They each climbed in, and she groaned and pressed her head against the steering wheel.

"I'm sorry," she said. "I told them I was bringing a classmate over to work on a project, and I told them you were an android, but . . ."

"You didn't tell them who I am," Reid guessed.

"My stepdad has dealt with your brother and his friends," she explained. "It's how I knew who you were."

"Like I said, I've heard it all before. I'm used to it."

She looked up at him. "Yeah, but you don't deserve to be treated like that. *You* haven't done anything wrong." She swore under her breath. "This is why I just wanted to take photos at the school."

"We could have, for yours at least," Reid said. "Why bring me here if you knew?"

"You showed me something personal. I guess I wanted to do the same." Alyssa looked out the window. "If I had known he would react that way—that either of them would act the way they did—I never would have—"

"It's fine," Reid insisted, and before he realized it he'd grabbed her hand. He was surprised by how warm it was. It was small too, in between both of his. He'd never really touched a human before.

Alyssa froze, but she didn't pull her hand away. She stared down at their interlocked hands, then looked up at him. Finally she squeezed his hand with hers and turned to place both her hands on the steering wheel.

She cleared her throat. "Let's get you home."

As they pulled away from the house, Alyssa chattered away, obviously trying to keep things between them lighter than they had been. But as Reid stared out the window, he couldn't stop flexing the hand that she'd squeezed. He swore he'd never felt that kind of warmth before.

7

ALYSSA

The next couple photos for both Alyssa and Reid went without incident, mostly because they didn't go back to Alyssa's house again. She noticed that Reid didn't invite her over to his home either, but she wasn't going to push about it. She didn't know much about android culture, though she did know many of them didn't like humans. She figured it was easier for him to just keep her separate from that part of his life.

For Reid's third photo, he brought her to one of his favorite photography locations—a dock on a small lake just outside of town. It was another place, he'd told her, that he'd never brought anyone to before.

Alyssa decided to shoot her third at the park where there was a tree that she and her friends used to climb when they were kids. She hadn't tried to climb it in years, but when Reid bet her she wouldn't be able to anymore, she couldn't resist trying to prove him wrong. Her third photo wound up being a shot of her sitting on one of the lower branches with a look on triumph on her face.

When she told him she wanted to title the photo *Girl Proves Superiority over Boy*, Reid was sparked into climbing the tree himself. She told him he was cheating since he was so much taller and had a clear advantage, but he joined her on the branch and forced her to pose for a selfie with him. The shot showed her glaring at the smug look on his face.

"What's that photo for?" Alyssa asked. "We already took mine."

"Yeah," Reid said. "I just wanted the photo." He'd already started the climb back down, so he didn't see the blush that crept up her neck and face when she heard that. It took her the entire climb down to regain control over the corners of her mouth that seemed intent on forming a grin.

* * *

Alyssa was still having trouble keeping the grin from her face when she came home that evening, but it was wiped away clean when she walked into the kitchen and found her parents waiting for her.

"Hey," she said carefully as she dropped her backpack onto the kitchen table. John's arms were crossed and he was scowling, while her mom's eyes kept darting back and forth between the two of them.

"Were you out with that android boy again?" John asked.

"He has a name," Alyssa said, "and you know what it is."

"They're just working on a school project together, John," her mom said.

"I don't like her being out doing who-knows-what with him given everything that's been happening lately." He walked over to Alyssa. "You don't see what I see on the streets every day, honey. These androids are dangerous. They're violent. They don't know how to behave in our world yet."

"Not every android is like that," Alyssa said with a glare. "Reid isn't like that."

"His brother is."

"Well, he's not his brother! He doesn't even hang out with those guys. He doesn't like being associated with Derek." As the words came out of her mouth, she realized she'd said too much.

John narrowed his eyes. "Just how much are you talking to this android?"

"I don't know," she said. "We talk in class and when we're working on the project. He's my friend."

Just then, her phone buzzed on the table. Before she could snatch it up, John's eyes darted down to see Reid's name flash on the screen. John's nostrils flared. "He has your phone number?"

"It's just so we can meet for our project," Alyssa lied.

"And what if this brother of his finds your number?" John asked, his voice rising. "If Derek Black finds out you're the daughter of a cop and he finds your number in that boy's contacts, he could—"

"It's not like androids have cell phones, John," she cut in. "The messages go right into their heads through that AndIP program. And I highly doubt Reid's brother is going to *hack into his brain* anytime soon . . ."

"I don't care! I don't want you spending time with him unless it's in class," John snapped. He turned away from her. "End of discussion."

Alyssa's jaw dropped. She looked to her mom to say something, but she could tell that her mom wasn't about to come between them in this. Alyssa grabbed her things and stomped into her bedroom.

She didn't care what her parents thought or said. Reid was her friend. She liked spending time with him. There was nothing they could do to stop her.

8
REID

For Reid's fourth photo, he asked Alyssa to
meet him in the park in his neighborhood
on a Friday night. Most androids didn't go
to the park very often yet, as the concept of
enjoying nature for the sake of enjoying it was
still a bit unfamiliar to them. But Reid liked
spending time there. He wasn't surprised to
find the small grassy clearing was empty when
he arrived.

"Hey," Alyssa said behind him, a little
breathless as she jogged up to him. "Sorry, I told
my parents I was going to see a movie with a
friend, and I stopped to buy a ticket just in case."

His eyebrows raised. "You went to all that trouble? Why?"

"So I can leave the ticket stub in my trash." She shrugged, trying to look casual.

"Your parents check your garbage can?"

"I don't know, actually," Alyssa said. "But John is a cop, so you never know. And this way if they go snooping around, then I'll have some evidence."

"I don't understand," he said. "Why do you have to do that?"

She breezed past him, grabbing the camera bag from his shoulder and striding through the cool grass into the clearing. "So what are we doing here? Taking some kind of artsy nighttime shot?" she joked. She was clearly avoiding his question.

Reid decided he would let her—for now. "Not many of us come here," he explained. "When we moved into the neighborhood, it was the biggest surprise. None of us had ever lived somewhere with a space just dedicated to trees and grass and the earth. It's a very . . . human concept."

Alyssa grew quiet as he spoke. She pulled the camera out of its bag and looped the strap around her neck.

Reid looked up. They were far away enough from the city lights, so the stars gleamed brightly against the black of the night sky. "Sometimes I like to come here, to remind myself."

"Remind yourself of what?"

"That even with the most advanced technology, the most developed AI science has ever seen, we're still so small compared to all that," he gestured up to the starry sky. "My brother loves to talk about how superior we are to humans. He thinks it makes him significant. I'm okay with being insignificant."

There was a flash of light in the corner of his eye. After a couple seconds, he turned to see Alyssa crouched on one knee with the camera angled up at him.

"*The Glory of Insignificance*," she said quietly. He smiled at the title.

Alyssa moved to get up, but before she could Reid dropped to the ground beside her.

He grabbed the camera from her and put it away, then stretched his legs out in front of him.

They didn't speak for several minutes, each taking in the quiet sounds throughout the park—the gentle breeze stirring the trees, a small stream trickling, the crickets chirping in the taller grass. Without even thinking about it, he knew there were four crickets total. If needed, he could have told Alyssa exactly how far away each cricket was from them and the note of each chirp.

"I can see why humans like this," Reid said. "It's . . ." He struggled to find the right word.

"Peaceful," Alyssa finished for him.

"Peaceful," he repeated. Yes, that seemed fitting. He nodded. "I understand the value of having parks where people live."

Alyssa laughed, and he looked at her in confusion. "You say it so clinically. Like it's a math problem or something—trees plus people equals happiness."

He didn't exactly understand what she was getting at.

"Sometimes, there isn't an explanation or an answer," Alyssa told him. "Something is just . . . right."

As they looked at each other, Reid experienced a series of unfamiliar feelings. His mental processing went blank. His breath quickened. His palms warmed.

He could hear Alyssa take in a sharp breath, and he wondered if she was going through the same thing. He was about to ask her about it, when she leaned forward and pressed her mouth against his.

Five seconds. It felt like much longer, but that was all the time it took before she pulled away. Reid's lips instantly felt colder. Had they always been this cold?

Alyssa's eyes blinked open, and Reid realized he hadn't closed his. She gave him a shy smile. He wanted to return it, but he was still so confused. "What was that?" he asked.

Her eyes went wide. "You . . . you don't know what a kiss is?"

"No, I do. I just—androids don't really do that," he said. "But, why did you?"

Her cheeks went red, and she sank back. "I thought—did you not want me to?"

"It's not that." He didn't really know how to answer that question. Kissing wasn't something that came naturally to androids. How was he supposed to know whether he wanted her to kiss him or not?

"Did you not like it?" she asked quietly, almost a whisper.

He thought back to how warm her lips had felt on his. How his mind had cleared when he'd looked at her. They weren't unpleasant feelings, just . . . unfamiliar. New. Different. "I guess I don't know," he said, wanting to be honest.

She looked devastated, and finally he got it—*she* had wanted to kiss him. He knew enough about humans to understand that meant something. *She has feelings for me?*

"I'm sorry," Alyssa said. She stood quickly.

"Wait." He grabbed her wrist and scrambled to stand up with her. She kept her gaze down when he looked at her. "I just—you have to help me," he said. Despite his advanced mind, it had still taken him this long to fully understand what was going on between them. How Alyssa felt about him. But now that he did, he didn't want her to think he didn't want it. He'd seen human relationships in film and TV before. He'd seen human couples walking together in school. He knew what Alyssa was expecting.

It wasn't that androids didn't have relationships. But, in comparison to all the others, *this* human emotion was the most complicated to understand. And maybe that was the point.

He took her hand. "I've never done something like this before. It's all pretty new to me," he said.

"Do you not kiss in your . . . culture?" she asked.

"It's not that we're incapable of it," he said. "But, no, I guess it's not often done. I've never kissed someone before."

That made her grin. "Well, for starters," she said, "you can put your hands on my waist—here." She pulled his hands so his arms were wrapped around her, and she rested hers on his shoulders. She rolled up onto her toes.

As he lowered his face toward hers, she whispered, "And this time, close your eyes, you weirdo."

9

ALYSSA

They didn't have plans to hang out the next day, but Alyssa was still feeling so giddy from the night before that she didn't stop herself from texting Reid to shoot her fourth photo. She figured that was a good enough excuse so she didn't seem *too* overeager to see him again.

And even if she did, she didn't really care because he replied almost immediately that he wanted to see her too.

Alyssa looked at herself in the mirror and wondered if her parents would be able to notice any difference in her. She just couldn't stop smiling. After a few more minutes of kissing

Reid, she'd forced herself to go home before her parents would get worried. The last thing she wanted now was for them to figure out what was going on between her and Reid. She could already see the look on John's face if he found out what had happened last night—and that had been just kissing.

She told Reid to meet her at the school's track. It didn't really mean much to her, it was just the first place she'd thought of where they might be able to spend time without anyone seeing them. *Track and field is a spring sport, so no one will be there in the fall, right?*

She didn't need to tell Reid that they would have to keep this thing between them a secret. Or why.

"It's better this way—for now," he said as they walked around the track. "If my brother or your stepdad found out . . ."

"I know."

When they'd walked a full lap around the track, they paused so Reid could take a photo of her. He didn't ask her why they came to the track. Maybe he didn't need to. Alyssa didn't know what she would title this photo, but she decided she didn't care. Maybe she would call it *An Excuse to See You.*

They started another lap, and this time Alyssa pulled Reid's hand in hers. She watched him look at their hands as she laced their fingers. "Never done this before either?" she asked.

Reid shook his head. "I think my parents do it, though."

"So, androids marry for love then? It's not, like, an arranged thing?"

"I guess it depends," he said. "As far as I know, yes. Most android couples are together because they want to be together. Because they"—he lifted their joined hands—"feel something for each other."

"So you *do* know what a relationship is then," Alyssa teased.

He scowled. "It's not that I didn't know what it was," he insisted. "I'd just never been in one. I've never done any of this before."

The look he gave her made her stomach flutter.

"Does this make you my girlfriend, then?" he asked.

Alyssa laughed and leaned up to kiss his cheek. "Only if it makes you my boyfriend."

* * *

They spent the next two weekends hanging out at the school track because Alyssa was right— no one came over there during the fall. She played him music by her favorite bands on her phone. He told her what it was like growing up in the tiny plywood house his parents had built themselves. She told him how her dad had died.

When they were at school, they tried their best to keep their distance. They worked on assignments in their class together, and they made sure not to linger at each other's lockers. They didn't sit together at lunch, but they texted the entire time.

They kept forgetting to take their last photos. They had other things to talk about instead.

The third Saturday they came to the track, Reid grabbed Alyssa's knit hat after she had said something sassy to him and held it high above her. She was jumping up and wrapping her arms around him to try to reach for it when she heard, "Alyssa?"

They both turned to see Austin walking toward them, his face red and shiny and his hair damp with sweat. He was wearing his football practice pads.

"Austin," she said, stepping away from Reid. "What are you doing here?"

Austin's eyes darted from Alyssa to Reid to Alyssa again. "Practice." He gestured behind him in the direction of the football field. "Coach needs an extra bin for a drill, so he sent me over here to check the other equipment shed."

She turned behind her to see the school's other shed, usually used for PE classes. She hadn't realized the football team practiced here over the weekends and could have kicked herself for it. How had she not thought about that?

"Is there a problem?" she heard Reid ask and turned back around to see Austin watching him suspiciously.

"Nope," Austin said. "You know, we've got one of you on our team now. I don't know what Coach was thinking." He laughed meanly. "If you ask me, we should keep to our things and you all should keep to yours."

"Yeah, well, no one asked you," Alyssa snapped. "We have to go finish our project." She pushed Reid to start walking, wanting to get as far away from Austin's curious looks as possible.

10
REID

That Monday, Reid had the distinct sense that he was being watched. During the first two passing times of the morning, he couldn't figure out where it was coming from. It wasn't Alyssa, because she had been texting him for most of that time and would have said something. He tried to shove the feeling aside, telling himself he was imagining it.

It wasn't until third period let out that Reid was certain something was going on. He'd just gotten to his locker when a hand slammed into the closed locker next to his.

It was Austin.

He leaned in to the locker and crossed one leg over the other, seemingly casual as he smirked at Reid. He wasn't as tall as Reid, but he was stocky and muscular. Reid knew Austin would be tough to go up against if it came to that. He'd never gotten into a fight before. He wondered if Austin had.

"What do you want?" he asked.

"Just wanted to come say hi. See how your little project with my neighbor is going." Reid didn't need to be an expert in human behavior to know Austin was lying.

"Fine." He opened up his backpack to load in materials for his next class.

"Seems like you're spending an awful lot of time together on it," Austin continued. "Shouldn't you be wrapping up about now?"

"It's a semester-long project," Reid muttered. "The whole *point* is to take the full semester."

"Whatever," Austin said. "Why don't you—"

"I heard you got benched because of that *new player* on your team," Reid interrupted. "Too bad."

Suddenly Austin snatched Reid's backpack and chucked it to the ground. He stepped up to Reid and snarled, "Shut up, you stupid droid. Why don't you mind your own business and stay away from Alyssa."

Reid clenched his jaw. "We're just working on a project together."

"I saw you two on Saturday, all cute and cozied up together."

Reid knew he shouldn't give in to Austin's taunts, especially when they were about Alyssa, but he couldn't help it. "I understand if you're jealous . . ."

Austin's nostrils flared and he shoved Reid. "I'm not jealous, you little—"

"What's going on over here?" came Mrs. Murphy's voice.

"Austin!" Alyssa shouted, coming from the other direction. A crowd had formed around them, and she had to shove past people to get through. She raced over to them as the teacher pushed both boys away from each other.

"It's nothing," Austin said. "I was just reminding Reid here to keep to his kind."

Whispers traveled through the hallway as everyone looked from Reid to Alyssa. Her cheeks went red, but she stood tall.

"Austin just doesn't like that Reid and I are working on our class project together, Mrs. Murphy," Alyssa said hastily.

If Mrs. Murphy understood what was really happening, she didn't let on. She just pursed her lips and said, "Every partnership in my class is an android-human pairing, Austin. That's the nature of the class, same as yours."

Austin opened his mouth to retort, but Mrs. Murphy looked down at her watch. "Passing time is nearly over. Get to class—all of you!"

As soon as she finished, the first bell rang.

Realizing the fight wasn't going to happen, the other students wandered in the direction of their next classes. Alyssa stood beside Reid, glaring at Austin.

Austin sneered at both of them. "We'll see what John has to say about all this."

As he stomped off, Alyssa turned to Reid. "Are you okay?" She rested a hand on his arm.

He noticed Patrick standing a couple feet away from them, his fists clenched as he watched Austin walk down the hall. Reid hadn't even seen him before, but he had no doubt Patrick would have stepped in if Austin had tried anything more. When Patrick finally looked over at them, Reid quickly pushed Alyssa's hand away.

"I'm fine," he said. Alyssa seemed to notice Patrick now too and took another step back from Reid. "Talk to you later. I have to get to class."

As he walked away from her in the hallway, Austin's words rang through his head. Reid quickly sent a message to Alyssa. *He's going to tell John.*

Her reply flashed into his mind almost instantly. *I'll figure something out.*

11
REID

Reid trudged into his house at the end of the
day, so ready to be away from that school. His
parents were both gone, and he was thankful
for the quiet.

"Hello, little brother."

He turned to see Derek sitting on the
couch, clearly waiting for him. Derek didn't live
at home anymore, so he was here for a reason.

"What do you want?" He didn't have the
energy to jump through hoops for his brother
today.

"I heard from a reliable source that you got
into a fight with a human today."

"It wasn't a fight. It was just . . . an altercation."

Derek wasn't having it. "What was this *altercation* about?"

"Nothing."

"Really? So some random human just came up to you for no reason and wanted to start something?"

Reid rolled his eyes. "Obviously you know that's not what happened. I know the human—he's nothing to worry about. He doesn't like androids."

"I've heard as much," Derek said. "But it sounded like there was more to it than that. Something about a human girl?"

Reid sighed. "Is this coming from Patrick?"

"Don't worry about it."

He looked out the window, avoiding his brother's gaze. "I told you, it's nothing. We have to work on this project together, and her next-door neighbor doesn't like that we're partners."

Derek scratched his chin. "That doesn't sound like nothing. I don't want this human causing problems for you. You know where he lives? I'll go over and talk some sense—"

"No," Reid said. "Don't go near her."

Judging from how silent his brother had gotten, Reid knew that was the wrong thing to say. His hands gripped the windowsill as he waited for Derek to say something.

"Reid, tell me about the girl," his brother said slowly. His voice was too controlled.

"What's there to tell?" Reid said, trying to sound casual about it. "We were partnered up at the start of the school year to work on this project together. She's a human. My age. I don't know . . ."

"What's her name?" Derek asked.

"Why do you want to know?"

Derek slammed his fist on the table next to the couch. "Enough. Tell me *exactly* what is going on with this girl."

"Why should I?" Reid snapped, whirling around. "She has nothing to do with you!"

Whatever Derek was looking for, it was clear he'd found it as he looked into Reid's eyes. He sat back and crossed his arms.

"I knew it. You have feelings for this human."

"I don't know what you're talking about," Reid tried one more time, but he knew it wasn't convincing.

"I've heard of android-human relationships happening before, but I never imagined one of my own would be *stupid* enough to actually do it," Derek said. "A human girl? Really? What's wrong with the androids at your school?"

"Nothing," Reid insisted. "I didn't mean for it to happen—neither of us did. It just . . . did."

"You know what they've put androids through, Reid. How could you betray your own kind by being with one of them?"

"She's not like that! She defended me to Austin today, and she's gone up against her stepdad too."

"So her parents don't approve?" Derek asked teasingly.

"They don't know. But her stepdad doesn't like me. He—he knows who you are."

Derek chuckled. "I'm that well known among the humans? Good. Let them be afraid."

"No," Reid snapped. "He knows about

you through his job. And if you would stop causing problems and getting into trouble with the human cops, then maybe Alyssa's stepdad wouldn't—"

"Wait a minute," his brother interrupted, "is her stepdad a *cop?*"

Reid didn't say anything, but Derek still had his answer.

"You end things with that human girl right now."

Reid glared at him. "You can't tell me what to do."

"If you know what's good for you, you'll listen to me," Derek said, his voice getting louder. "Those humans are dangerous. They're selfish. They only look out for themselves— and that human girl is *certainly* not going to look out for you when her daddy comes down on her for being with you."

"You don't know anything about her!"

Derek just stared at Reid, as if he didn't recognize his own brother anymore. Then he stood up. "Come with me. I have something to show you."

"I have homework," Reid insisted. He had no interest in going anywhere with his brother.

But Derek wasn't having it. He grabbed Reid by the arm and dragged him toward the front door. "This will be educational, I promise."

* * *

Derek brought Reid to his run-down house in the other side of the neighborhood. There were fewer families in this part of town— most of the androids who lived there were like Derek. They were against the combined society and made little effort to interact with humans. Because of that, most of them had trouble finding work outside of the android neighborhoods.

For the first couple hours, Reid sat by himself while Derek and his friends hung out. Patrick and his brother were there. They mostly bragged about fights they'd gotten into and trouble they'd caused for the humans. They complained about the human cops who patrolled their neighborhood. Reid had tensed at that, worried Derek would bring up Alyssa's stepdad. He didn't, but he stared down Reid while the others complained of all the wrongdoings the human cops had inflicted upon them.

Reid knew some of the human cops were too aggressive. They were rough on innocent androids and hardly paid attention whenever any of them needed help. And of course he would rather have an android police unit working in their neighborhood instead, but he knew that not every human police officer was a bad one. Just like not every android was a troublemaker like Derek.

By the time the sun went down, Derek and his friends were ready to head out. Nobody would tell Reid where they were going, but they dragged him along with them as they walked to the edge of the neighborhood. Reid tensed. He didn't exactly know what they did when they went out on nights like this, but he had a feeling it was nothing he wanted to be a part of.

The border between their neighborhood and the human part of town had turned into a bit of a no-man's-land. There was a block or so around the entire neighborhood that didn't belong to the androids and didn't belong to the humans either. As far as Reid had heard, nothing good happened there.

"Derek," he said, coming over to his brother. "Come on. Let's just go back to the house and hang out."

"Relax, little brother." Derek swung an arm around his shoulders.

Reid was just about to tell his brother he wanted to go home, when he heard a familiar voice down the street.

"Well, well, droid, looks like you have friends after all."

Reid turned to see Austin and a half dozen other human guys with him. Austin was holding a wooden baseball bat, and Reid could only imagine what the others had with them. Austin took in Derek standing next to Reid and said, "I take it this is the big brother we've all heard so much about."

"Austin," Reid said, "get out of here. Now." He didn't like the guy, but that didn't mean he wanted him to get caught up in a brawl with his brother.

"You must be the piece of garbage who's been harassing my brother," Derek said.

Austin grinned wickedly. "Hey, it's like I told him. We just want you all to keep to your side of town, and we'll keep to ours."

"And yet you came all the way to our neighborhood," Derek said.

"We're just here to continue our friendly chat from earlier," Austin said. His friends spread out.

Reid looked from Derek's friends who had joined them in the street to Austin's friends who were coming closer, and he knew this was not going to end well.

12

ALYSSA

Alyssa woke to the sound of her alarm blaring. She silenced it, then shoved her head back under her pillow. Her eyes felt puffy and tight. Her fight with her parents the night before came flooding back to her.

Austin had gone to the police station and told John about her and Reid. She knew he didn't know everything, but apparently whatever he'd said had been enough for John to leave work early and come right home. He'd barged into the kitchen and demanded that she end things with Reid immediately. Her mom, startled both by the outburst and the fact that

Alyssa was now dating Reid, tried to get them both to calm down, with no success.

John barked that he was going to call the school and force them to pull Reid from Alyssa's class. She could consider their project over, he'd said. And she was to never see Reid again.

Alyssa, of course, insisted that she would do no such thing.

Her mom had tried to suggest that they have Reid over for dinner, so they could get to know him first before making any decisions about her dating life.

John wouldn't have it, though, and said he would rather eat cement than have "that android boy" in his house one more time.

It turned into a screaming match between Alyssa and John—the biggest fight she could remember them ever having—until John finally told her she was grounded until she agreed to end things with Reid. No phone, no social activities, no TV, no internet. All she could do was go to school and come home to sit in her bedroom until she agreed to his terms.

At that, Alyssa had slammed her bedroom door so hard the nails in the doorframe came out of the wall.

She groaned at the memory and scrubbed at her face. At least she would be able to see Reid at school. *Nothing John can do about that,* she thought to herself happily. *It's not like he can keep someone out of school.*

She showered and dressed, and as she was coming out of the bathroom to get breakfast, she heard her mom speaking quietly on the phone. That was unusual, so Alyssa stopped just outside the kitchen to listen in.

"Three fractured ribs? I can't believe this. Austin is such a nice boy," her mom was saying. She was quiet for a moment, then said, "No, I haven't told her anything yet—"

"Told me what?" Alyssa asked, stepping around the corner.

Her mom jumped. "Oh, I have to go. Call me if you hear anything else." She turned to Alyssa and gave her a smile that was too wide to be reassuring. "Good morning!"

"Mom," Alyssa said, "what's going on?"

Her mom fiddled with the phone she held in her hands. "That was John. He doesn't want me to tell you yet, but I'm going to. But"—she held up a hand—"you have to sit down, and you have to promise me you're going to stay calm."

"Mom, you're freaking me out," Alyssa said as they both sat at the kitchen table.

"Apparently, Austin got into a fight last night. He's in the hospital with three fractured ribs, a concussion, and who knows what else, but he'll be all right."

"Okay . . ." Alyssa knew there had to be more to it than that.

"And—" Her mom took a deep breath. "The fight was with some androids. I don't know the details, but Derek Black and his friends were there. A couple of Austin's friends got hurt, and Derek and some of his friends were too. They're all going to be okay, but John said it sounds like Reid was there."

Alyssa's breath caught. Her hands began to shake.

"And," her mom said slowly, "he's missing."

* * *

Alyssa stayed calm as she promised her mom she would. But it was only because she was freaking out internally and knew that if her mom saw that, she'd make her stay home from school. So she forced herself to funnel her emotions. She managed to express the right amount of concern, enough to be believable yet not cause her mother to worry.

She picked at her breakfast but didn't eat much. She put on her shoes, grabbed her backpack, kissed her mom goodbye, and got into her car.

But she didn't drive to school.

Instead she drove through town until her eyes had teared up so much she could no longer see the road. She pulled over on a random street and cried until her throat hurt. She might have stayed there all day if it weren't for the random lady knocking on her window and asking if she was okay. Alyssa assured her she was and wiped the mascara streaks from her face.

She couldn't sit here anymore. She had to get out of this car. She thought about going to the tree where she'd brought Reid, the best place she could think of to get away.

And then it hit her.

There was no guarantee, but she had an idea of where Reid might be.

13
REID

He heard her footsteps before he saw her. She was practically sprinting over to the picnic table he was sitting on at the abandoned drive-in.

"Oh my god!" she panted. "You're okay. Thank goodness you're okay."

Alyssa wrapped her arms around Reid and tucked her face into his neck. He brought his own arms around her, pulling her close. He could feel her heart pounding. "What's going on? Everyone thinks you're missing."

Reid nodded slowly, feeling like his mind was underwater. "Yeah, I didn't go home last night."

"I heard what happened. Are you hurt?" She stepped back to look at him. His cheek was throbbing and his hands were scratched up, but other than some bumps and bruises he was fine. After he realized he wasn't going to be able to stop the fight from happening, he'd gotten out of there as fast as he could. "Reid, your parents must be worried sick."

"I know," he said. She was right. He'd gotten multiple messages from them throughout the night, but he couldn't go home yet. He had too much to think about after what had happened.

"What's going on? You're scaring me."

"Sorry. I've had a lot to think about."

Alyssa's forehead creased at that, and she joined him to sit on the table. She moved to loop her arm through his, but he pulled back.

A look of hurt flashed across her face, but she didn't say anything. She folded her hands in her lap and waited for him to say something.

Reid took a deep breath, then said, "All of what happened last night was because we wanted to be together."

"Look, I know Austin was a jerk, but I don't care what he thinks—"

"It wasn't just Austin," Reid snapped. "My brother found out about you. About your stepdad."

Alyssa tensed.

"He's not going to do anything," he assured her. "But he told me I had to end things with you. And when I said no, he brought me out to . . . I don't exactly know what he planned to do, but we ran into Austin and that's how the fight happened."

He let out a heavy breath through his nose. "So, after I got away last night, I came here and just thought about everything. Everything that's been going on the past year, everything that's been going on since this started between us." He shook his head. "If this is what happens when we're together, then I don't see how we can make it work. Not when this is how people from either side react. Not when *you* could get hurt."

"So that's it?" Alyssa said. "I don't get a say in it? You don't want to fight for us to be together, so you're over it?"

"I *did* fight for us to be together, and look what happened!" Reid hissed.

"Yeah, well, so did I," she said. "I got into the biggest fight of my life with John, my parents took away my phone and everything else, and I'm still here trying to make it work."

Reid threw his hands up. "And that's the kind of life you want to have if that's what it means to be with me? You live on lockdown at home, not speaking to your parents, and my brother could come after you at any moment?"

"If it means we get the chance to be together, then yeah," she insisted. "I don't want to end things just because everyone else has a problem with it." Tears filled her eyes, and she angrily wiped them away.

"Alyssa, I'm sorry," he said, keeping his voice firm even as his throat closed up. "We can't. It's too dangerous."

"Don't say that!" she shouted. "If you want to end things, then tell me you don't want to be with me."

She was the first person who'd made him feel this way. But if this was the only way to keep Derek away from her and her family, then it was worth it. At least that's what he told himself.

He looked her in the eye and forced himself to say, "I don't want to be with you anymore."

14

ALYSSA

The next week passed in a blur. Alyssa was so upset that her parents gave her back her phone, not that it made her feel any better. Reid wouldn't respond to any of her messages. He avoided her in the hallways at school, and he started ignoring her in their class. Whatever their assignment was for the day, he completed his share alone. When she tried annoying him into speaking to her, he moved to sit with Patrick and his partner. When she told the teachers that he wasn't working with her, he stopped showing up to the class entirely.

When the last bell rang that day, Alyssa

barely even heard it. She was tired of feeling this way, of feeling like she had no control over the situation. As she gathered her books at her locker, she decided it was time for that to change.

She found a group of android girls she recognized from her Android/Human Relations class standing in the hallway. She'd only spoken with them a handful of times, but they all seemed nice.

"Hey," she said quietly. The girls turned to her in surprise but greeted her pleasantly and smiled at her. For a moment, Alyssa felt guilty that she hadn't taken more time to get to know the others in her class besides Reid. She resolved that, after she got her issues sorted out, she would reach out to them again. For now, though, she simply asked, "Do any of you know where Derek Black lives?"

* * *

Alyssa didn't know what to expect when she pulled up to Derek's house, but this was not it. The yard was well kept, despite the run-down state of the house. A couple of androids were sitting on the front step, laughing together.

She forced herself to keep her head high as she walked up to the house. The androids stared at her but said nothing when she approached. The main door of the house was open, but there was a closed screen door. When she reached for the handle, one of the androids said, "Can we help you?"

"I'm looking for Derek Black," she said, happy that her voice stayed strong.

"Never heard of him," another android said.

She was so nervous that at first she thought she'd said the wrong name. Then she caught the way the others were trying not to laugh, and she glared at them. "I know he lives here," she snapped. "I'm—I'm a friend of his brother's, and I need to see him."

"Oh, so you're Reid's little human friend." The looks the androids gave her made her skin crawl.

This was going nowhere fast. "Fine," she said. "Don't help me then. You can just let Derek know that this human is going to sit here on his front step until he comes and talks. I'm sure all the other androids on the street will *love* seeing that he hosts humans in his own home."

Finally, she heard a chuckle from inside the house. "Wow, you don't let up, do you?" She turned to see what looked like an older version of Reid step to the screen door.

"Derek?" she asked.

He arched an eyebrow. "Quick for a human, I see." He opened the door and jerked his head, signaling that she should come inside.

She followed him in, hoping it wasn't a mistake to go inside where no one would be able to hear or see her. Still, she tried to keep faith that her plan would work.

Derek slumped onto a ratty couch and gestured for her to sit across from him in an old recliner. "Sorry we don't have finer things here," he said. "There's only so much provided to us, thanks to your *caring* people."

She wasn't going to fall for his obvious attempts to egg her into a debate with him. "I'm not here to talk about your furniture," she said. "I'm here to talk about your brother."

"Oh, really? Come to ask for his hand?" Derek teased.

She narrowed her eyes. "I've come to tell you that you can't bully him into not being with me."

Derek laughed. "I can and I will if it keeps him safe. I know all about your dad and his cop buddies. I've seen firsthand what they do to my kind. What do you think would happen if you and Reid got into an argument? You don't think your stepdad would send the squad cars after Reid?"

"No," she said. "Just like he wouldn't do that if I had a human boyfriend."

"Well, see, that's the issue," Derek said. "I know how your people treat androids, and I'm not about to let my little brother get sucked into your world for that."

"Why not try to make positive change? Reach out to humans and start a better relationship?"

Derek crossed his arms. "That's easy for you to say, coming from your safe, human part of town."

Alyssa squeezed her eyes shut, growing frustrated. "That's not—this isn't what I'm here to talk about. I can't change your mind about all humans, I know that. But I want to change your mind about me. I want to be with Reid. And he wants to be with me, but he's too scared of you to stand up to you."

"That's too bad," Derek said. "Makes you wonder why you even want to be with him, doesn't it?"

She huffed. He was even worse with the games than the guys outside. "Fine, if I can't change your mind about humans in general, and I can't change your mind about me, then at least think about your brother. If you do force him to do this, aren't you worried he'll resent you for it?"

Derek just laughed. "That doesn't bother me."

"I don't believe you," she said. "Not when I know how much you care about him."

"Oh, really? And what would you know, little human?"

"I know that you risked taking him to a human drive-in movie theater when he was a kid, even though you knew it could be dangerous, just because it was important to him," she said.

Derek stopped laughing. "He told you about that?"

"I don't know you, like, at all. I've heard the worst kinds of stories about you—and I'm sure at least some of them are true. But I have to believe that someone who cared that much about his kid brother doesn't just stop caring."

Derek was quiet. He leaned back in his seat and crossed his arms again. "Even for a human, you're pretty annoying."

"Yeah, well, even for an android, you're a real jerk."

He laughed again, then looked at her for a long moment, clearly thinking. "You really want to be with my brother?"

She nodded.

"And he, for whatever reason, wants to be with you."

She didn't know what to say to that, so she said nothing. Her silence seemed to unnerve him more than anything.

Derek rubbed his face with his hand. "Well, you're persistent, I'll give you that." She sat up. "All right, I'll leave you two alone—for now. But don't think I won't be watching."

Alyssa grinned. As she stood, he said, "And this doesn't change my mind about humans—including you."

She kept walking and said over her shoulder, "We'll see about that."

Alyssa practically skipped to her car. She drove away quickly, eager to get away from that house. When she got home, she texted Reid to tell him she'd talked to his brother.

You did what? he sent back. She didn't want to give all the details over the phone, so she asked him to meet her.

But minutes turned into an hour, and he didn't reply. She left her phone in her room during dinner, hoping she would come back to find a message from him. Nothing.

She fell asleep that night watching her phone.

15

ALYSSA

When Alyssa walked into their Android/
Human Relations class the next morning, she
didn't know what to expect. But she certainly
didn't expect that Reid would skip again.
In fact, he didn't show up to school at all that
day. She thought about texting him again
to see if he was okay, but she started second
guessing herself.

Maybe he *didn't* want to be with her
anymore. Maybe the time apart had been
enough for him to get over it. This was his first
relationship, after all. Maybe he'd decided he
didn't want to deal with human emotions.

She couldn't stop thinking about it as she drove home from school, feeling just as confused as she had been when she'd left that morning. And when she got out of the car, what she saw made her feel even more confused than ever.

Sitting on her front step was Reid.

"Um, hi," Alyssa said as she walked up to the front of the house. "What are you doing here?"

"Hey," Reid said. "Sorry I never got back to you yesterday. I had to take care of something first."

"What?"

The front door opened behind them, and her mom said, "Reid, honey, are you sure you don't want some lemonade or something?"

They both turned to look at her, and her mom grinned. "Oh, you're home! Good! Reid has been waiting for you for nearly an hour." She winked.

Alyssa looked from her mom to Reid. "What's going on?"

"My brother told me what you said to him

yesterday," Reid said. "And if you're brave enough to face him, then obviously I had to do the same. So, I came over this afternoon and talked to your parents."

"It was the cutest thing ever," her mom gushed. "He came in and told John he's not going anywhere because he cares about you and—"

Reid coughed, and Alyssa almost thought she saw his cheeks flush. "Well, I think you get the idea."

Alyssa looked up at her mom again. "So, everything is okay now? With John?"

"He'll need some time, but we both appreciated Reid coming to talk to us. We just want you to be happy, sweetie. That's all we've ever wanted." Her mom smiled down at her. "We can talk more later."

She closed the door, and Alyssa joined Reid to sit on the front step. "I'm sorry I just ended things like that," he said. "I really thought I was doing the right thing."

"I know."

"Can I kiss you now?" he asked, and he

looked so nervous about it that Alyssa had to laugh.

When they pulled away from each other, she asked, "So what now?"

He grinned. "I believe we have one more photo to take."

16
REID

They decided to take their last photo in front of the school building. These photos had turned into a timeline of their relationship, and AI High had brought them together in the first place.

It was the end of the semester. They sat together on a bench in front of the building while Reid tried his best to hold up the camera in front of them. "You know, this would work better if I could just use my tripod," he grumbled.

"Yeah, but that's not a true selfie!" Alyssa insisted. "And since you won't let me take it on my phone, this is a compromise."

"We are not finishing our project with a potato-quality photo from your crappy phone."

"Hey, this is a new phone! It came out, like, last year."

"Yeah, and it still makes my AndIP messages lag."

"Well," she sniffed, "maybe your AI is what's potato quality here."

"Okay," he said, "let's just take this already. It's taken us several months to get here as it is."

"Yeah, hurry! I'm super cold." Alyssa rubbed her hands together and blew onto them.

"Hmm, that doesn't seem to be a problem for me, despite my so-called potato-quality programming."

Alyssa just grinned up at the camera as he held it above them. Reid wrapped an arm around her. The camera flashed, and she already knew what she would title this one.

How We Got Here.

ABOUT THE AUTHOR

Loren Bailey is a writer and editor in Minneapolis, Minnesota. She enjoys adventuring, baking, binge-watching Netflix, and spending too much time on the internet.